I0750184

Poetry by AC Benus

Hymenaios, or The Marriage of the God of Marriage
A Classical style myth in 2,600 lines of Blank Verse
ebook: ISBN 9781953389091; paperback: ISBN 9781953389084

Summer 2020 – Hell in a Handbasket
A contender for the Pulitzer Prize in poetry, 2021, this collection grapples with the year of pandemic, racial justice and environmental crisis
ebook: ISBN 9781953389015; paperback: ISBN 9781953389008

The Thousandth Regiment
A Translation of and Commentary on Hans Ehrenbaum-Degele's War Poems "Das tausendste Regiment"
ebook: ISBN 1657220583; paperback: ISBN 9781657220584

A Man in a Room and other poems
Poems written when AC Benus was 21 years old
ebook: ISBN 97817345103; paperback: ISBN 978173456107

The Easiest Thing in the World
And other poems: marking the third anniversary of the Pulse Nightclub attack
ebook: ISBN 9781734561029; paperback: ISBN 9781734561036

Rima Fragmenta, or Fragments of a Rift
Fifty Sonnet for Kevin
ebook: ISBN 9781734561005; paperback: ISBN 9781734561012

First Love: Poems for Ross
For everyone's first love, both bitter and sweet
ebook: ISBN 9781734561081; paperback: ISBN 9781734561098

One Hundred and Fifty-Five

AC Benus

an AC Benus Impression
San Francisco

Grateful acknowledgement is here offered
for the support and encouragement
I've received on the literary site
www.gayauthors.org.

ISBN 978-1-953389-11-4 (ebook)
ISBN 978-1-953389-10-7 (paperback)
ISBN 978-1-953389-12-1 (hardback)

ONE HUNDRED AND FIFTY-FIVE SONNETS FOR TONY

Cover photo:
Artem Aaranin / Pexels.com

Library of Congress Control Number: 2021907498

Sonnets
for Tony

Lyrics of Dedication

And so here, this work I offer

Has found a form, and is complete –

For you, dear one, I proffer

An infinity of Love's heat.

Many will be the hearts kindled,

In the centuries that follow,

Where Love grows not to be dwindled,

But venerated as hallow.

I love you, Tony; now I've said it,

And quatrains living in my blood

Will always make your beauty sit

Like heaven's dome with stars bestud.

Sonnet No. 1

You touched my heart, with that thing you did –
Taking your laptop just to chat with me,
Sitting at your family event like a kid,
With a private smile, everyone could see.
Risk; Fear – You moving in the shadow of fright,
Typing that you just had to take it out –
And perhaps in me, you sense the daylight
Coming to cast away all your self-doubt.
It moved me because it took some planning –
To bring your laptop to this party indeed,
And keep the date on which I was counting –
That appointed time and hour we agreed.
    Public/Private, what we do is for us,
    For you and me, what we hold is precious.

Sonnet No. 2

Hollow the feeling, destitute the art
To try to put into words what it is
That has made me queasy right from the start –
But then again, oh what magic is his.
A word, a thought, a kind gesture given,
And all over again, I fall once more,
As if for nothing else I've ever striven
Than to make him happier than before.
So my art of feelings may be bereft,
So my heart of wisdom may be new stripped –
But for love of him I'll suffer no theft
Of the loving passion that my soul has gripped.
    To hold onto, or to let loose in time,
    These are the only choices, that are mine.

Sonnet No. 3

In my mind's eye, you lie within
The snow-white crispness of your drifting bed sheet –
You're spread on your tummy, as I begin
To lift and let the sunshine your body meet.
My hand slides to caress your lower back,
Over skin that makes silk blush too warmly,
While under me, you rouse with feline knack,
And your arms pull me down so wantingly.
Yet, what is art, if not some sort of failure –
For if I can see you, and feel you here,
Can others come to grasp your total allure,
Stretched on poor words only I might hold dear.
    But, Hesiod said matter is made to live
    Only when Love comes, and His sweet blessings give.

Sonnet No. 4

Sometimes I feel like the sand on the seashore,
Soaked and crushed and relentlessly ground down –
To the point where I can bear it no more –
But then, you wash over me, and I'm unbound.
If I could, I would cup your soul gently,
Like a scoop of seawater to hover
Near my head, and pour on me completely –
One infinity to wash the other.
For it is only time that is the wave,
That comes and goes and sadly leaves behind,
The crushed substitute that we make our grave
With the ever finer moments we find.
    Not so with Love, for It is the water
    That grinds Time to dust, now and forever.

Sonnet No. 5

Boy, lie with me, your head on my heart,
So you hear the stillness you engender –
You've said you're no poet when we're apart,
Yet, listen to the strains you render.
Right side/Left side, there's harmony in bed,
With the two of us making up the whole,
For we lie metaphor to all that's said,
About two bodies with one conjoined soul.
So love me as the phoenix was consumed,
To rise again, not in cold sophistry,
But fired by Love's flame, and never doomed,
For you are Poet, to all my Poetry.
    You the left wing, and I the right, will rise
    To shine in this, in many future eyes.

Sonnet No. 6

The ancient legend you asked me to tell,
Of how Apollo lost his precious boy –
How a jealous West Wind Hyacinth fell,
And sent a god to his knees from lost joy.
But why must so many of 'our' stories
Come to tragic or unhappy ending? –
Because 'their' wicked mind often glories
To break the unions they find offending.
Yet, sometimes in the past we've won,
And still to this day on Mount Olympus,
A king and his boy love as they begun,
With Ganymede pressing his cup to the lips of Zeus.
    For if we are brave enough for our fate,
    Only happy endings for us await.

Sonnet No. 7

The rain hits the windshield and upward streaks –
While the miles stream by, you are on my mind,
And the hollow loneliness in me speaks
Of the words of yours that are less than kind.
Why talk of these things that are hard for me –
Of a future you may have beyond my sight,
Of a poor deceived wife and family,
When both you and I know it won't be right.
The little drops are like stars, or like tears,
And form a slow-motion constellation
That glows briefly before it disappears,
Taking with it all hope of salvation.
    Say you'll wipe those words away like the rain,
    And condemn none of us to lasting pain.

Sonnet No. 8

I kneel on the chair you are sitting at,
And though the miles that split us are many,
Real is the head I now tilt as we chat,
And strong is the kiss we share as any.
It seems you are reading my thoughts; and more –
You reread and interpret them well,
So my wants and feelings you don't ignore,
And 'my magic' takes you in like a spell.
Enchanted that you just want me happy,
I think myself unable to resist,
And although I know it may sound sappy,
Just tell me what greater love can exist?
    No matter the miles; no matter the words,
    Real are the bonds that link us as one inwards.

Sonnet No. 9

I close my eyes, and feel you on my skin –
You lie me on my back before the sofa,
Then, tenderly, with your hands you begin
To lift my legs on the seat, and tell me: "Ah."
You will take the clue; you will be in charge,
For I will be the clay that you will mold,
And press, and work, and your hands will enlarge
A new heart for me to replace the old.
Back on the floor – feeling you and your touch –
Your love is a moving experience
That rocks me to my core, and means so much,
My eyes close from being delirious.
    Love in perfect balance can quickly cede,
    And let the other roughly take the lead.

Sonnet No. 10

Without trying, you become my stanza –
    My rhythm, my rhyme, my metre beating;
    The wanderlust of our two hearts' meeting;
Like the calm strain of an Italian romanza.
Yet, why indulge me in this extravaganza –
    My heartache, my pain, my sorrow fleeting,
    When all should be light and my joy heating,
Like the burning comfort feel of silk organza.
    But music of the mind and heart are one,
    As the brain gives up to let love win –
    For these resting beats not to be outdone,
    They must start again right where they begin,
    Yet, without you, my heart and mind find none –
    While with you, my soul finds its fun within.

Sonnet No. 11

Bobbing along the rays, your summer commends,
Like a hand raised to the currents of air,
That laughter and jokes among you and your friends
Will shake off inclement weather for fair.
Riding so, if in your fun's tumult,
A wayward grin should happen to slip –
An enigmatic; an inscrutable bolt;
A little gesture that plays on your lip –
Then your friends will see, but they won't know why.
The deep-rooted genesis of your smile
Frees your hand from the open car to fly
So your thoughts can be with me awhile.
    Revel in the face of all that sunshine,
    And make the summer jealous you are mine.

Sonnet No. 12

Hopelessly I take what little you give,
And like the needle of a balance scale,
Shift between the calm and provocative –
But then, you're under me in stunning detail.
Your whole body in motion – a ballet
Racked and contorted in pain and pleasure –
Your closed eyes open on mine, as if to say:
"Your love's more to me than I can endure."
So then, in that movingly simple thought,
My wrong doubts vanish and I am returned
To the equal poise tween which I am caught –
Halfway mad, feeling half-way loved and spurned.
    But later, rest with all my love your pillow,
    And I will weigh me out in your pleasure's glow.

Sonnet No. 13

Rising from the pool, water dots your skin,
While your body wet and shining is like
A pure sheet of glass, making my head spin,
And my troubles you effortlessly strike.
At that moment pause internal/external –
How we look and what we feel near and far –
For time stretches the temporal/eternal,
Making what we will be, now what we are.
Your flesh is a million faultless round mirrors
Reflecting back to me a love perfect,
But dull are they to the smile that endears,
And of the future makes me recollect.
    With my mouth I will scoop the drops seen there,
    And bring them to your lips for us to share.

Sonnet No. 14

A sham, a botch, a wreck is all my work –
As it comes tumbling down about my ear
To ring like cracked bells that my duties shirk
Each time I try to say what I hold dear.
Failure stalks my door as a hungry wolf
Baying: "Never good enough; never good..."
And it makes me tremble within myself
To think that I will never be understood.
Yet – somehow – through the tears that are welling,
A little thought can come to comfort me,
One that is a budding beyond all telling,
Namely, that all my words are ones you'll see.
    For through my grief, I know you will read them,
    And Love can graft onto your swelling stem.

Sonnet No. 15

You love to lay into me like chocolate,
Before and after, you tell me the same,
That my skin savors of it; your favorite,
For it is enough to drive you insane.
Yet, when I am down; when I am unwell,
Your healing hands take that hurt unto you,
And our common suffering you dispel,
As if it were the least that you could do.
But I never want you to be in pain,
I want to overwhelm all your senses
With goodness and light, because it's the arcane
That you bring to me with your caresses.
    So slide your hands, and melt me with your touch,
    Like the chocolate, I know you love so much.

Sonnet No. 16

The way champagne bubbles crawl up a glass,
The way stars etch the dome of the night sky –
In slow motion, all the wonders amass,
And in my cloudy brain your thoughts magnify.
The feel of your fingers on my body,
The feel of your kisses over my ear –
Your rippling voice calling me your 'daddy…'
Makes me fall as if through the atmosphere.
While bubbles may be near, and the stars far;
The one within my grip, but not the rest,
My hold on you is like a shooting star,
For the wish I make is better than the best.
    Thinking of you is like effervescence,
    So, near or far, I can taste your essence.

Sonnet No. 17

I love every aspect of you. Your mind
Is like a faceted jewel in sunlight
That no matter which way I twist I find
Refracted rainbows, crystal clear, and bright.
Then I consider your body, and how
My hands cup you in richness like the Earth –
Like I scoop sensual soil right now –
As dark and brooding as we were at birth.
And so I am brought to your soul, for it
Is no captive to light, or dirt, or time –
For as long on the world as we may sit –
It will be my model of the sublime.
  Every day they mix anew and then form,
  Love as the element I can transform.

Sonnet No. 18

Fear is a blind thing – hands before the face –
Black velvet rippling through a starless night;
Which way up; which way to a state of grace –
How dependent we grow upon our sight.
Yet sometimes I think worry is a gift,
Given to sharpen joy to a focus,
So that even from the darkness we lift
Ourselves with our weak hands from the abyss.
I know you have fears that I long to calm,
And they call out to me in clarity,
Like David's voice entreating God by psalm,
To end black nights of their austerity.
  So reach out your hand to me, dear boy,
  And I'll lead you where we can live in joy.

Sonnet No. 19 [1]

That Romeo loved Juliet is true,
But equally Mercutio loved him,
And how the tragic tale a twist could do,
If the boys could love, and sadness betrim.
Rick loved Ren, and "In the Flesh" they could be
Back again, redeemer to each other,
Despite all the world's cruel hostility,
Their eyes beheld risen Love without cover.
So despite how the temporal world may try –
To hold down, and suppress, our worth –
We will always be there to refute their lie
That our greatest gift wasn't given at birth.
　　Love me: that is all of you I can ask,
　　Make them feel we are worthy of the task.

Sonnet No. 20

Click; stop: click; stop: the hands of time go on,
Rigid soldiers, their arms stiff and marching
Have limited moves in the game matching –
Still; stymied: hands; jerking: the clock seems pawn.
And yet, all our hopes and dreams on it fawn,
Begging for enough time dispatching,
To render our longings some detaching,
And beef up our resolve with brawn.
　　But none of that really seems to matter
　　When I simply think that I see your hand
　　Lifting to my lips like heaven's ladder
　　And pressing there so we both understand
　　Nothing in the human heart is gladder
　　Than to have time greater than grains of sand.

Sonnet No. 21

That little sadness in you beats like a clock –
Telling the numbers that minutes hours count
In the slowness of misery's tick-tock –
When time stops and waits for sorrows to mount.
But if I could, my hand would wipe the slate
So all that reckoning would mean nothing
And know I would, I shall not hesitate
To offer your heart a little soothing.
Do not be sad, dear young man that I love,
Within our hearts a timeless strain now beats,
One that gives measure to everything above,
And makes quick the dead wherever it meets.
    Your sadness cannot keep up with that pace
    When Love renews all of our missing grace.

Sonnet No. 22

The pudge-face God of Love may pull his bow,
And finger his darts with a lusty aim,
But it's you who draws tight my shaft below,
To prick me surer than that boy of fame.
For these lines are meant to make you smile,
Although the weather may be oppressive,
If these words on your lips tarry a while,
Then sweeter than chocolate is what you give.
We need a little romance in our life;
A bit of a break just to reconnect –
With paper hearts and bon-bons to kill strife,
For you as my Love, I'll always select.
    Though it may be far from Valentine's Day,
    Be my summer Valentine, in every way.

Sonnet No. 23

Your voice is the voice of an angel, but
The tone of which makes the temple rock,
For scripture says both church and tomb will strut
To a trumpet call, and the world restock.
But when your fine treble sounds in my ear
The future opens 'fore me like a book –
The story of which will end every fear
To confirm my path is the right one took.
So what matters if the stones themselves shake,
And everything that had substance once
Will reconcile and find itself awake,
Though with blinking eye, we'll all look the dunce.
 But in that moment, I will also know,
 It was you who called me, and will gladly go.

Sonnet No. 24

Standing at your open window, I see
You bathe the sultry summer night with sighs
And only those born of anguish can be
More tormented than hell with all its lies.
You are lost, you feel your orbit is fixed
By the locking grasp of some heavy hand,
Strangling by the evils they enlist,
And stymied with all things they demand.
But in the night's warm, let yourself surrender,
For even then, I will be with you still –
If sad, then two hearts will grow tender;
If glad, four eyes will drink the stars their fill.
 God gave us hearts so we could love and feel
 Joys and ache on His scale of hurt and heal.

Sonnet No. 25

Your silence speaks louder than any word.
The white screen before me, is blanker than death.
So in wiped quiet I can be deterred,
And feel lifelessness has taken my breath.
Yet, there's nothing I can do about it,
For tears mean nothing to a wall's coldness,
And that's all I see here – from where I sit –
Despite determination and boldness.
Fear is in the stillness as well as in the scream,
The cry can let you know, when quiet takes all.
But tell me all is not as it may seem,
And that this man is not in for a fall.
    Your tears, your anger, your pain I can take,
    Just don't tell me it's my heart you might break.

Sonnet No. 26

My days are oddly slow and empty if
I have no prospect of talking with you;
Without it I pray and worship your gift,
And if it's gone, I don't know what I'll do.
You often say that I have everything –
That you have nothing in this world but me –
And that sorrow bites at me like a sting
To comfort the smart and thereby set you free.
But my days, my hours, my nights are not
The sole property of me anymore –
I bid you use them and know that you've got
Enough to keep you from being poor.
    With your love, I have everything that I need;
    Without it, God help how this heart will bleed.

Sonnet No. 27

To think that you in your sadness welter –
As if through it you had to go alone,
When all the time I would provide shelter –
Makes me wail like a penitent's atone.
You think of yourself as a two-wheeled cart
Where one axle is resting on the ground,
And the more you pull the more it will start
To scrape and cry and make a terrible sound.
But what you don't know, what you do not feel,
Is me on the other end lifting up,
Like a mother hefting a car of steel,
So that her trapped child can crawl and get up.
    If you trust me, I will halve your burden,
    So you'll never have to wallow again.

Sonnet No. 28

How I long to create the simple phrase –
"Compare thee to a Summer's Day," or then
"Some Glory their Birth; Some their Skill" amaze –
So that all can know I love you from my pen.
I long to draft that perfect line they will
Quote and read and whisper to their loved one
In all attempt serious to fulfill
The debt of love their beloved has begun.
In some time with "Those Darling Buds of May"
Other eyes and other hearts will quote you
As dimly reflected in what I say,
In my attempts to render you life-true.
    Better than any Summer's day will be,
    The future that quotes my dear love of thee.

Sonnet No. 29

I lay my head down, and I close my eyes –
The room about me may be dark and still,
But flashes of your thought makes me realize
More than stars in the universe can thrill.
At one level, you and I never part,
And haven't since the time our hands first joined
To stamp the other's image in his art,
And find that Love, has been perfectly coined.
Upon all the starry wonders of you,
My eyes close, but actually open
In my darkened room so the light bursts through
Leaving my lips uttering an "Amen."
    What force can light up every darkened night? –
    That which you impress in me with your sight.

Sonnet No. 30

Can a person's heart concave and convex –
Twisting an image over to and fro
To ever re-mint it fresh, and then sew
On the mind's mirror, where an engrave reflects?
Like feelings that both behave and perplex,
Convoluting the clear path as they flow,
So my thoughts of you, dear boy, come and go,
But deep within me an enclave collects.
    Limpid runs the gentle underflowing
    Your smooth currents bring to my state of mind,
    And like Narcissus to the water's ring
    The beauty is beguiling that I find,
    And no distortion is there reflecting
    One love mirrored by two faces of kind.

Sonnet No. 31

Quantum theory has it that we can be
Both here and there; where our touching becomes –
Within the space smaller than we can see –
The superstrings' glowing music that hums.
At the level where you and I are thus
Indivisible – not made of matter,
Nor worry or heartache – our animus,
The energy of love, sings the patter.
In the state living in the in-between,
You and I are undivided and shall
Never be cut by Time's knife, which is keen
To sever Earthy bonds so physical.
    In the realm where we have never parted,
    Our touch is here and there, right where we started.

Sonnet No. 32

You hard-pressed with loneliness in your room
Turn over all; uproot what you possess,
Tossing socks and CD's within that gloom,
Till all outward signs resemble a mess.
Within, we all wish to be together
With clear-cut organization which says
We are calm, cool and collected, whether
We are tormented throughout our own days.
So, you stand in the storm you have made,
Gathered around you the outward signal
That isolation is hard to make fade,
And that even hope is transitional.
    But in such chaos, let me pick you up;
    Let love show how to undo the blowup.

Sonnet No. 33

Why do we have a brain, if not to think –
Why a heart, if not to have it broken,
And so common wisdom would have us sink
To the state that nothing can be spoken.
Frustrated and sad that *they* can't let us be;
That a boy-loving boy is no big deal,
And there's no point in denying what they see,
That people join because of what they feel.
So if I ask you to take my hand now –
So if for your love I ask forever,
Will you sanctify blessings to avow
That love is love, despite all endeavor?
  Heart and mind, the universe in us beats,
  And in measure all enmity defeats.

Sonnet No. 34

You bring comfort to an unquiet soul;
Your pillow is the sail that me protects
To luff back under your watchful control
A rocky mind, cliff-faced with impending wrecks.
You ask me to tell how much I love you –
I say, as the sky loves the rising air;
As birds the currents holding them move through;
As Justice loves for all things to be fair.
The down of my dreams is what I may sleep on,
But next to you, I soar above the crags;
If my eyes hold your image as my sun,
I will sail to where our hope never flags.
  I love you as God should everyone,
  The perfect love beyond comparison.

Sonnet No. 35

Leander kissed all over by Neptune
Had no room for doubt swimming the Hellespont
That the love on his lithe body bestrewn
Said the god made no mistake in what he want.
So sad to think the majority rules
Say the past must change and be sanitized,
And that those who loved openly were fools
Whose private lives should not be scrutinized.
But, Alexander had his Hephaestion,
And side-by-side long years of war campaigned,
Never once held his love in hesitation
To say the gods had a mistake ordained.
    Love's always certain, despite others' views;
    It can change their hearts, though their minds refuse.

Sonnet No. 36

I think a pair of eights are you and I –
A mark others see but can't comprehend;
A linking amplitude to signify
That like-energy into one can blend.
Infinity flows – one to the other,
Never fading; never diminishing –
Always fresh that we may discover
The Alpha and Omega's beginning.
For the cipher's key is written in sand –
The "open sesame," a word soft-spoken,
And your lips upon my own can then band
The tie between us never to be broken.
    For it is Love which unlocks realities;
    Its eight-ball foretells all possibilities.

Sonnet No. 37

Despite the struggle, the strain, the effort,
Nothing intimidates like a blank sheet,
Simply because of what it can support,
If I get it right, and not incomplete.
The truth is, it's late and I am tired –
I ache within to speak with you now,
And perhaps I'm more sad than inspired,
Knowing that's the one thing Fate won't allow.
So I strain with pen, and struggle with ink
To drive the sleeplessness away by will,
And maybe selfishly in me I think
You have your own blank spot with me to fill.
    Thus, connected by desire, and pain too,
    "Good night, my love" might be the best we can do.

Sonnet No. 38

Come with the stillness of a cat, and lace
Hallow fingers quietly through my hair,
Then lie your chest full on my back in place,
To pin me as your captive then and there.
My eyes will open in the dreamy sight
Of your arms coming round to press my lips,
And the urge to kiss your flesh I won't fight,
Feeling your full weight settle on my hips.
Move my hair; kiss my neck and ear, and please
Tell me the words to open my portal –
Whisper them with assurance and with ease,
And slip off the bond that says I'm mortal.
    Open up my passage with your measure,
    Like Sinbad's cave spread rich with treasure.

Sonnet No. 39

On an island jagged by crystal blue waves,
A boy's body drips coming from the sea,
His tones falling like drops on musical staves,
Saying no more perfection can ever be.
Your smile is like the cant of a sunbeam
To sidelong strike and dazzle where I stand,
But warmer than any starlight can seem
Is the way it lights my body, face and hand.
Venus was born from these waters way back,
And rose from the glinting sea a diamond,
But striding before me, there's nothing you lack,
For the facets of you won't be outdone.
    You are my jewel within the sunshine's glow,
    Murmuring light to colors deep below.

Sonnet No. 40 (2)

Alone and pensive over the lonely countryside,
I measure my paces both late, and dragged rigidly,
and to my eyes holding out, set to bolt, intently
at the sight stamped in the gravel of a human stride.
No other weapon but fight-or-flight is fortified
in the view of my fellow men, who evidently
ascribe joylessness to my actions generally,
and have no idea how I blaze on the inside.
    But from now on, I vow these mountains and hills will dote,
    these waterways and woods will know in me they strengthen,
    and indeed, will see what hidden from others shall brim.
    For no matter the harshness of the path, or remote,
    wanderer no more, that Love won't leave my side again,
    motivating, reasoning with me, and I with him.

Sonnet No. 41

Like a man sitting in an empty church,
A whisper about me reverberates,
Filling dark recesses as if to search
The holy voids where His light hesitates.
If I fold my hands in prayer and watch them,
I see one hand mine and the other yours,
And if from my muttering mouth prayers stem,
It's our commingled voice that then endures.
Lonely and separate as we are right now,
The sacred emptiness is just your soul,
And I inhabit that space somehow,
Knowing even your absence can console.
    Still, I whisper your Name and Love at once,
    And two forces soar and the gloom confronts.

Sonnet No. 42

Oh my boy, the autumn seems to come on,
With each day a little less light than last,
While a bit more bleakness greets every dawn,
Whose grayness tries to say summer is past.
But the days themselves are bright and sunny –
I have you and your smile to keep me up,
And although it might sound somewhat funny,
With you my day also seems to windup.
The sunsets come sooner with their chill,
And inch-by-inch the day is given to night
To longer make my sleep and dreams until
I once again can behold you in my sight.
    Autumn portends no misery this year,
    No chill wind will touch me if you are near.

Sonnet No. 43

For you, all my thinking seeks out a rhyme;
For you my heart beats in pentameter,
And for this I may want only time
To say I'm more than a poetaster.
But like the mark of infinity though,
The terms go round and round without decrease,
Building greater density and then so,
Like light from an atom my soul release.
Your fuel for my flame will never go out,
Feeding my hope as a sacred motet,
Although for just the right word I cast about,
You'll always be there to call me your poet.
    So in words I may seek the rhythm and rhyme,
    And joy that they are yours, and that you are mine.

Sonnet No. 44

Where you are staying, fountains rush and reel,
Shards of water fill rainbows in the air,
And as you stand and watch, freshness you feel –
On your body – but inside, you despair.
The water is like the attitude
You show the outside world: sharp and pert,
But as your bubbles fall in multitude,
That evanescence only bares your hurt.
But within our inner life, you and I
Retain the deep stillness like a mirror
Where one can recognize his own sigh
Reflected in the smile he holds dear.
    Turbid the outer world and its demand;
    But deep within, unruffled by any hand.

Sonnet No. 45

I wish to break the cycle; give you something
You could show your friends and be proud of –
A token to say for you I am your king;
That showers you with the happiness of love.
I'll tell you of the happy time ahead
When hand-in-hand over green grass we'll go,
While our sorrow we'll replace with joy instead,
And in our hearts' honeymoon we will glow.
The day your hand slips into mine for good
Will be the day I freshly see the world,
For all its pain will be understood,
And the true banner of you and I unfurled.
    Let your friends read this, and let them smile
    That you're passionately loved in style!

Sonnet No. 46

Loneliness can take to it a sharp point –
Twist it 'round the blade, and shavings fall
In ribbons thin-sheared away to the viewpoint
That there was ever company at all.
Today the freshness of the morning's eye
Rises this Sunday peacefully around,
And with each passing word wants to know why
I ignore her and her beauty profound.
But Nature can't see, She's the blade that cuts –
Trims my life by minutes and days that fade,
As these lines sharpen, if I have the guts,
The simple point I have not yet made.
    I'd trade all the future mornings right now,
    If I could just say "I love you" somehow.

Sonnet No. 47

Perhaps the truth of it is rarely said,
But the highest form of concentration
Comes not from torment or racking the head,
But rather arrives as relaxation.
So the sea may crash against stone boulders,
As starlight waves lap the tides of the Earth;
For every force its energy transfers,
Though greatly diluted in its real worth.
Thus for a meditative state I strive,
But the thoughts of you go crashing my skull;
Bathing my soul so that I might feel alive,
And open arms to catch your miracle.
    With eyes closed I can feel your force relax,
    As it washes over me in climax.

Sonnet No. 48

Delta waves are spiky and aggressive,
The length to do business in, but the scale
Ascends ladders to the contemplative
Where the frequency meets God's without fail.
The morning breaks upon my sleepy room
To find me working as if in a dream –
Perhaps on the day I will be your groom
My mind will burst forth like every sunbeam.
But until then it is the alpha wave,
Closet to dreams and meditation,
By which I can gather you and save
My deepest love for your benediction.
    Though the outside world is harsh and cruel,
    To think of you is to be spiritual.

Sonnet No. 49

The body of every person alive
Emits a tiny amount of light,
Which is destined to shine and to thrive
Totally below the level of sight.
Some say this light is like that of a star,
And as old as when the universe burst;
Others that it is the mind's avatar,
Showing connection clairvoyant first.
But a third way might prove the middle ground –
That the light from us made the cosmos part,
And gave meaning to all dead matter found,
For without Love, creation could not start.
    The light I behold in you is just the same
    As shone on us before the world had a name.

Sonnet No. 50

Time flows ever towards an evening-side
Sweeping hopes and wants until they recede
Back to the stymied calm that they precede
To wash away all in its waning glide.
But like water, time has its morningtide
Swelling and lifting up every misdeed
To the point that truth might at least succeed
To roar fire by a dull ember's side.
    But those coming and goings, my dearest,
    Can't effect the steady pace we have built,
    As we stroll holding hands on the clearest,
    High path above the current and the silt,
    For the way we've chosen is the holiest,
    And will never float away on tides of guilt.

Sonnet No. 51

I've had a vision of a future time
When this world will be mired in cruel war;
Wallow in pollution and sink in crime;
A time when both trees and men die rank at core.
They will look back at us and demand to know
How greed and apathy played such a part
When we recklessly let everything go,
Saying the future will be state-of-the-art.
But a beacon shines in my vision too,
A hope, and also an absolute –
A want that none of my foresight will come true;
And a faith in mankind that's resolute.
    For eyes yet unborn, but reading these words,
    Will know Love as we did ever afterwards.

Sonnet No. 52

Some structures are built of marble and brick,
Others of arching concepts, and of grace;
A Parthenon look of entasis slick,
Or unseen constructs of the commonplace.
Unit by unit these inner stones click
To lift us to what we most desire,
And there curses all that's shallow and quick,
To build something that matters; that's higher.
Though palaces are built for the heretic,
It's the love we lay down one for the other,
One good thought at a time, that's politic,
To build masonry that will not smother.
    A spirit finds its greatest pride of place
    When love has laid out and measured the space.

Sonnet No. 53

Regimes and their monuments may tumble,
World events may sweep the cobblestones clean,
And sluttish Time with her wheel fumble,
Rising *him* up, to clear that man from the scene.
Sometimes I'm woken from a cold sleep by
The intense presence of your lips upon
My warming flesh made hotter by your sigh,
Saying my work won't to the future be pawn.
For although overturned statues may be downed,
Pulled to the ground by hopeful hands cocksure,
The soaring arches in us won't be found
By bitch Time's wrecking ball, of that I'm sure.
    For the love we build is beyond all strafe,
    And the hearts yet to come will keep it safe.

Sonnet No. 54

Gold is the flesh of the gods, we are told –
Incorruptible, never to tarnish –
But gold too are the bones of love that's bold,
Holding spotlessly straight our deepest wish.
A king was buried with a simple prayer;
An inscription that his eyes may behold
A million years of happiness from there,
And that his serenity be multifold.
So at times I wonder what is Death's lair;
What is it like to slowly lose this life? –
To die with a mummer of the unfair,
And feel the tether cut by shadow's knife.
    But despite the end that is temporal,
    Our gaze is already golden and immortal.

Sonnet No. 55

Tonight the blue sky is candied with clouds,
Which a sultry light wind blows to the east –
And in these vapors on the move are shrouds,
Sailing my affections on to your feast.
For I send along with them my sentiment
To seek you out in the lands that will be
Touched by morning's amber light occident
Long before it has a chance to see me.
If, when it finds you, my dearest young man,
Do not be surprised at how on your cheek
The clouds and dark azure meridian
Plant my kiss and strongly for me bespeak.
    Chase the dawn, oh my love, and find the boy;
    Lay him low with beauty, and my charms deploy.

Sonnet No. 56

You are like the automobiles of old;
Running deep, inscrutable like the Sphinx,
You purr through your smile, and do not withhold
Your claws that are as sharp as any lynx.
I am grateful I'm pet to your tiger,
And can run my hands from ears to your tail –
To feel your spine stiffen in sheer pleasure,
As amused snarls from your curled lips exhale.
You as my love are powerful and sleek,
A continual alertness in rest
That none can challenge, but we who are meek
Can have the thrill of stroking your wise breast.
    Riding in front of all is your mascot;
    Feline-proud, lovely and fiery hot.

Sonnet No. 57

Our physical world has its own consciousness,
Which at the tiniest level always stays
A grouping of lifeless particles that stress
Us philosophers into an active haze.
So when I shutter myself still and apart,
I focus my energy on you and feel
Your reciprocation is all of my art –
If some of these images can find appeal.
For if there's a thing called the God particle,
It's a piece of reality paused until
The glance of human love turns it oracle
And offers order unto the volatile.
Agnostic, philosopher, or simple bard,
It's we who must push God to be the vanguard.

Sonnet No. 58

Holy Wisdom has raised her lofty dome
Above vaulted arches for centuries –
Her archangel wings fly in polychrome
Over buried crypts that hell might appease.
From atop their shimmering gold lookout
Christ-like stares pity mankind far below,
And question if anyone is devout,
Or if God is someone we could ever know.
But in wisdom is also a question,
And humility marched with Him to the cross,
So marble and jasper may clothe the sin,
And thereby His intentions double-cross.
Though some will abscond Love's greatest teachings,
Others like you and I *live* His preachings.

Sonnet No. 59

We've heard it before, that love is a game,
But, I will always let you win because
The one thing I fear, that can't be the same,
Will ruin everything Love thinks and Love does.
Like pulling up to the kitchen table
To enjoy a family meal together,
We should seek a relationship that's stable,
And strong enough to last our forever.
You'll win, but chose the game you want to play,
And do not torment the man who loves you,
For there'll never be a question that I'll stay,
But, how happy will we be when you're through?
    Winner, loser – what matters in the end,
    If it's Victory's loss we must defend.

Sonnet No. 60

From the crucible of our loneliness,
Into two different molds were poured our fate –
You to suffer now; me to alleviate,
And help you every bad feeling depress.
From the same molten sadness we have access,
To the unmixed potentials that await –
To the joy we can anticipate,
As our two halves fuse and become seamless.
    So easy comes the time when hand-in-glove
    Our traits that are impurities will be
    Burned off like slag, and the time we dream of
    Will be a golden age for you and me,
    Where body-to-body we'll be but love,
    And glint valuable to all who can see.

Sonnet No. 61

However else I feel, you are my muse,
Waking me from a cold sleep by will
To draw some lines I know you won't refuse
If I'm able to show you a bit of skill.
For in my ships I seem to find no rest –
When asleep, my confidence is shaken,
Constantly roiling me with the best;
When awake, your love of me's not mistaken.
So, inspiration and challenge you stay,
My north-pulling magnetic loadstone,
Guiding my barque back to a Viking fray,
Where old shortcomings must beg for fresh atone.
    A fevered brain gets no comfort in sleep,
    When awake and active it dreams as deep.

Sonnet No. 62

My sadness has the substance of music –
A hundred variations on a theme,
Whose notes are mad, and whose tones are mystic
To start again just as the end would seem.
But your love for me's a perfect melody,
Sweet, and clear, and high, like a morning bird.
It comes to seek me out in my malady,
To awaken me with a trebling third.
For to rouse me in the freshness of your thought
Is to shake off dark night's gloomy rerun;
To start new with you and the time we've bought
Is magic tempo bright enough to stun.
    To your love's refrain, I am never deaf,
    But am soothed, as you climb your treble clef.

Sonnet No. 63

You are not a romantic person by nature –
So I guess the fifteenth of this month won't
Mean much to you as a simple creature,
So, I'll be nice, even if my crass reasons don't.
To some, half-a-year goes by in a flash,
A winking routine of ordinary –
Drudgery like a slave under the lash –
But for me, it's been quite the contrary.
Six months of tortured bliss and heavenly
Contact with you and your beautiful life
Has brought me joy and torment orderly –
And passion, to stoke my every strife.
    If you remember our anniversary,
    There will be no happier man than me.

Sonnet No. 64

Like dust settling through a sun-streaked space,
There is a quiet anticipation
Every time from air I conjure your face
To float before me in rapt flirtation.
Sometimes I think there's nothing like a book
To keep pressed a memorial long dead;
That every eye resurrects with a look
What's gone, but worthy enough to be said.
And so your visage comes quite unbidden
To glide and haunt me in my empty room,
But Love to us will not be forbidden
Though our memory will be consigned to doom.
    You are every leaf of my book falling,
    And your image fills my deepest calling.

Sonnet No. 65

My soul is a bubble about to burst,
Growing full with an iridescent sheen,
And over the surface, it is traversed
With rainbow-silver and aquamarine.
You fill me up to the point of release
By coaxing and teasing my poor spirit
And making it so my love finds increase
Beyond its ability to hold it.
So, like champagne fizz on your palate soft,
Know each little pop will be replaced there
By finer that can carry us aloft,
Beyond the currents of sparkling air.
    As two bubbles rising in the sunshine,
    We will fuse, and ultimately combine.

Sonnet No. 66

Love is a prism that refracts the light
And bends the loved one into his base parts –
Split into jewel tones he rises in sight
More gleaming than has the power of arts.
Sometimes with you, I have to use my hand,
Draw it up to my forehead to make shade,
Because your light is more than I can stand,
And when it burns brightest, I am afraid.
But the crystal pure that is deep inside
Filters out every harshness for my eyes
To show me the pure you and where you abide
Channeled into color that never dies.
    Rainbow arcs fleetly grace the sky in a storm,
    But prism bands live always in perfect form.

Sonnet No. 67

I take you in my arms, and you tremble –
At that moment I'm forced to remember
That when you say you love me with voice humble,
I'm the first to love within you stir.
You did not forget to mark the day we met,
So my fears were unjustified complete,
And had I voiced them we'd both be upset,
But, Providence blessed us to be upbeat.
That I am your first love is an honor –
And sends me to my knees as I kiss your brow,
For you my love, don't know what you're in for,
As I'll mark our anniversary, and how.
    Close your eyes and let your first love show you,
    He has experience enough for two.

Sonnet No. 68

Sometimes I wonder if I can even say
That yes, I know you well, for seemingly
You and I grow closer with every day,
Yet miss the other's most heartfelt, aching plea.
When you say I provide comfort, and that's all,
You do not mean to hurt me, but you do,
For I am in your deep connection's thrall,
Like a binder's stitch to you through and through.
But, it is only fair that we must learn
The way the other expresses his thought,
And not to interpret that as a spurn,
To strew the path ahead with dangers fraught.
    You say what you want, and in your own way,
    And in my heart, judgment I will defray.

Sonnet No. 69

Equality has a mark and symbol –
A brave set where curves and lines extend,
And their chance of meeting is not dismal,
For though separate, their motion is a blend.
I don't want any misunderstanding
To ever stick between us good or bad,
For Love's nothing, if not always mending:
A frown to a smile; laughter for the sad.
So sixty-nine must be you and I,
The perfect dance immortal, ever set
To chase and follow, and never die,
Where one energy fuels both in duet.
    Round and round we may go, but there breed
    Infinite Love for the other to feed.

Sonnet No. 70

Why is being Gay so goddamn fucking hard? –
What is the deal with 'them' to get over it,
And their smug sense of being 'normal' bullshit,
As they pity-fest us in their sad regard.
So why pretend such a pompous-ass blowhard
Any place in your life has a place to fit,
And that 'common' opinion matters a bit
When it just toughens us to be more diehard.
    I need them to keep their dirty-minded hate
    As a projection that shines on but themselves,
    For the years go on, and it is getting late
    To reason where their dank anxiety delves –
    But, then like a bubble, you alleviate,
    As your kiss drives all fear outside of ourselves.

Sonnet No. 71

Crystalline is your cruelty because,
For my one slip of tongue, you lash out with
A thousand stripes more than hatred does,
And a malice meted plain and therewith.
My error was never intended to hurt –
Though it did – but yours was aimed for my soul.
Did I warrant that level of desert,
Just 'cause I lost one moment of control?
I do not understand that much anger,
For it must have been seeded very deep
To vitriol-flash as it might occur,
And every abuse upon me heap.
    But a man can stand up, and take it all –
    If Love stands beside him, he will not fall.

Sonnet No. 72

Through the void we're told to believe as God,
Is there any apathy as damning
As the way you've run me over roughshod,
Or any faith cracked that's more alarming?
Trying to come to grips, I wash my face,
And the gritty burn feels like some relief
For my head roiling like a basket case,
Struggles to grip onto a new belief.
In the emptiness we're taught that's holy
My eyes lift up, and water cascades down,
But what to see except purgatory,
When every encouragement is a frown?
    There's no way to end this feeling except,
    Seeing it through the tears that I have wept.

Sonnet No. 73

Ringing hollow in the deep chest of Love,
My voice should not seem a consumptive thing,
To prove weakness by example thereof,
That my life's breath just hangs on by a string.
But, although the sound of me appears weak,
The bubbling spring from which my words must flow,
Is a torrent of passion, and not meek,
Though it races in me from far below.
If it rings false in your ear, then I fail;
If it moves not your heart, then I die –
For your breath of forgiveness cures my ail
By giving worth to my every sigh.
    What more to say, than it is forgiveness
    That needs resound by being bottomless.

Sonnet No. 74

Shards of protection like sparklers to scare
Some destructive deer or birds from the field
Have the opposite intent than to ensnare,
And so you forgive, but I don't feel healed.
It's not for us that time will be lacking,
For a love this great was not simply born
Through the machinations of one living,
And can survive a brief lifetime of scorn.
But in your heart, I know you love me more,
Though in chrysalis you may have bed it,
It aches to stretch its wings in new ardor,
And fly its full now, if you will permit.
    Love is a butterfly that must be free;
    Reborn, it outlives all catastrophe.

Sonnet No. 75

Love to ourselves is a gift, that you've said;
We make gift of it to ourselves to choose,
To look at with stagnant, hopeless dread,
And thereby all the best options confuse.
In many ways I treasure your laptop,
It is a lifeline and a link between
Those impulses you have to simply stop,
And your desires to me that careen.
You say ours is too beautiful to live,
But you know it has already survived
All the cruel torment a cold world can give,
And through our joined suffering it has thrived.
    You choose to love me every day, I know,
    And what links us can sorrow overthrow.

Sonnet No. 76

Your skin is like molten alabaster,
Pygmalion pure; I've whispered in your ear,
And your animation soothes disaster
That stalked us with lupine menace and fear.
For our Winter's Tale will be one of heat,
Where mistakes are set aside by firelight,
And feet and shoulders are bundled complete,
In peace and warmth to see us through the night.
To touch your purity, and stroke your skin,
Heals all wounds we think we have inflicted –
For the cover we wear clears us of our sin,
And flesh-to-flesh, Love's blessing is predicted.
    With hand on heart, from us dear life redeems;
    Love warms our numbness, and no more stone seems.

Sonnet No. 77

You stopped me cold in the supermarket.
You staggered me and I could not go on,
So I stood in the frozen food aislette,
My hand trembling upon my coupon.
You in your warm world far removed from there
Paused to consider how much you love me –
How you wanted your hands on my flesh bare,
And drove me mad for you in slow degree.
So the mundane gives way for the special,
For who in this chill place seeing me stop
Would ascribe an intense love mystical
When they cannot see you in the backdrop.
    Warm or cold, your love is always around,
    It catches me wherever I am found.

Sonnet No. 78

I open my arms, and you fit like a glove,
Your ear on my pulse, my hand on your head,
For this contact; this silence – this is love –
In spite of all the things we have said.
There is no word for forgiveness that works
Quite as well as the contact of our flesh,
And no absolution that respect shirks
When our lovemaking starts again afresh.
I kneel as I write this, almost in prayer,
Before the page that can sanctify this,
And through the early morning hour, I swear,
As you still sleep in bed, I love you Tony.
    Now to return to your side, and renew;
    My love's better example, through and through.

Sonnet No. 79

I know your anger stems from them, and so
If it flares inappropriately then,
I'll feel your heat of rough injustice go
Right past me and fly out to them again.
We will be for each other what we need –
Whether among Italian cypress trees
In Liguria's sunny and warm lead,
Or in more northern climes with wintry breeze.
Still, the one thing we can't, is let them win,
For rage is their weapon to keep us down,
And questions all love that is masculine,
But they only spread their own *disrenown.*
Sun-lapped shore we'll be to one another,
Peaceful retreat, one there for the other.

Sonetto N. 80

Il mio abbraccio ti aspetta,
ragazzo, principe focoso –
con il tuo sorriso estroso,
si è tutt'altro che timidetta.
E come i pastori di vecchia,
bruceremo ardente come Amor
tra le colline e boschi ancor
dove il nostro sogno sonnecchia.
    Vieni da me con passione,
    prendere la mano forte offro
    di dimenticare l'afflizione,
    perché senza di te io soffro.
    Lasciate che questa relazione
    futuro amanti decifro.

Sonnet No. 81

We tend to hold the truth as an absolute,
But we are only allowed what we can handle,
And the veil torn from some memories acute
Are too much, even though God's the vandal.
You entreat me to look into our past,
To answer some questions of who you are,
Yet such a backwards glance I must forecast
Will renew pain that's better kept afar.
To have the slate wiped clean, and then the veil –
Mended; redrawn in gentle Mercy's name –
Gives us new chances of which to avail,
And ensure our present won't be the same.
    Not to the past look, for that is not right,
    When our future we have now in our sight.

Sonnet No. 82

Me 'the priest,' and you the prince's son,
Watch the long orange shadow cast on the Nile
Of He who dies in the West to be redone
By Night's magic, and resurrect in style.
In this boat at sunset's hour, you recline –
Your back is pressed firmly into my chest –
And my hands grip your arms both strong and feline;
My lips whisper: "You're the one I love best."
For in that moment of hazy languor,
This love of ours was first set to the strain
Of a lonesome flute to sing my ardor
In notes so tender they yet here remain.
    Rest your back firmly on my heart, dear boy,
    The Sun will rise again to bless our joy.

Sonnet No. 83

In life I have neither fame nor fortune,
And my hope hangs on by an onion thread,
While to the pits of anguish I tailspin,
Wishing the piece of me that still cares, dead.
This is perhaps one I won't let you read,
For my despair has no place in your life,
And my only wish is for you to speed
Towards my love and away from your strife.
But – my brain's hurt and tired; it craves sleep –
If I had a switch to power it down,
I could let me crumple into a heap,
And recycle every sorrow and frown.
    Do you see what my tired mind says here? –
    It wants to rest, but can only when you're near.

Sonnet No. 84

Everywhere my mind turns, inspiration's there –
History, Physics, Religion and all –
Disciplines upon our love come to bear,
That make of me a rhetorical thrall.
Once you sent me a poem you'd written,
And you did so with an apology,
Yet, it proved that you are deeply smitten,
For no other field offered analogy.
No one had ever done that for me before,
So it almost brings a tear to me now,
As it said I am the one you adore,
And all your poetry on me endow.
    While outside worlds might help this inspire,
    Your love from the inside keeps me afire.

Sonnet No. 85

Around me, baking apples scent the house,
While outside, burning leaves smoke in the clear –
And the season to my mood is like a spouse,
For autumn is the coziest time of year.
But, now with you, my bundled warmth I'll share,
And chilled fingers will soon be warmed by yours,
As hand-in-hand we will walk anywhere
The bracing wind wends our steps out-of-doors.
The smoldering leaves and sight of orange pumpkin
Take me back to the joys of childhood,
And in my languor boots adrenaline
In a way that nothing else ever could.
    For this year I will see fall by your side,
    And as kids again, we'll ride autumn's tide.

Sonnet No. 86

There is such hubris and conceit in Man
That not even evidence is good enough
If it contradicts some arbitrary ban
Which pigheaded Will says it must rebuff.
The hets must take all of our past from us:
No tomb for ancient partners is allowed –
No room for out artists 'that' to discuss –
Wikipedia whitewashes in a cloud.
Our past for us is from hand-to-hand passed;
From soft word-of-mouth, and from heart-to-heart,
A lover to his beloved, so at last
Sacred knowledge with Love can never part.
    Let them refute *this*, all they want to try –
    Our love is real, and that they can't deny.

Sonnet No. 87

I want to leave my bitterness behind.
Dump their acrimony back in their lap,
And in its place, with you I wish to find
The inner peace from which we may both tap.
If a man can pluck an angel feather
By reaching up towards the divine one –
As he soars through the blue-sky Earthly weather –
Then with you I think my task's already done.
To touch you is to know angels exist,
And that they – manly – love humans in return,
For what else can explain what lifts the mist
When your smile burns away my every concern.
    Light as a feather on His righteous scale,
    Our love outweighs densest Hate's every travail.

Sonnet No. 88

If I close my eyes, do it – there – just so
My hands can enclose yours, and my lips
Can caress the back of your neck just below
The points where shirt collar your flesh eclipse.
But, that roving hand of mine won't stay still,
As over your waist and upper thigh grips,
An escaped moan of yours tells me that I thrill
When it settles in one place, and unzips.
My kisses sink deep along your tilting nape,
While backwards your arms raise sensual flips
To pull me deeper into your shape,
As my breaths, my touch, inhibition strips.
    Turn within my embrace and reward me –
    Kiss me, and word and flesh will ever be.

Sonnet No. 89

The white feather of imagination
Can be conjured as a symbol of faith –
From Seagull or Eros, its activation
Is meant to instruct like a spectral wraith.
But what happens when the down of an angel
Alights upon a human hand? – How soft
It speaks of the hardship, which Man befell,
That sent us to the Earth with our wings doffed.
Yet human angels live and breathe, I feel,
Ones divine with Love's great ability
To forgive – and in that thought – to heal
Mankind's innate strain of hostility.
　　My angel fell into my hands, it's true,
　　Your downy love gives faith in what I must do.

Sonnet No. 90 (3)

Come to my awaiting embrace, I bid,
My boy, my fiery prince mythical –
With your smile both stern and whimsical,
That I find anything but timid.
And just like the shepherds of old we'll number
To smolder hot as Eros, the Blind Child,
Between the green hills and the forests wild,
Where we'll find our placid dreams aslumber.
　　Come to me dear boy with all your passion,
　　And take the strong hand that now I offer,
　　To forget all your pain and affliction,
　　Because without you, it's I who suffer.
　　Let the quality of our relation
　　Dear lovers in the future decipher.

Sonnet No. 91

Nothingness is the Alpha/Omega,
For what started in a Big Bang one morn,
Must end in a Big Crunch parabola,
Where creation dies to then be reborn.
Three quarters of our world is beyond sight –
Dark matter, or darker energy yet,
Exerts its force on us as sure as light,
While all of Time's veiled secrets it has kept.
But – there's one law darkness knows nothing of,
The strength animate that began it all,
For what has life that exists not in Love? –
Not touched before Time was primordial.
 So between us there exists a state of grace;
 Explosive and contracted as all of space.

Sonnet No. 92

Break the holy numbers' seal on the book,
For the fairest Vedic knowledge is free
To he whose motive is of pure outlook,
And whose love is of the highest degree.
'Conservation of knowledge' has it said
That darkness can never consume the light,
But by absorption, the Void's base is fed
To never lose what is simply lost to sight.
And so in sorrow's density and hole
I feel a mighty gravity luring,
But it's never one your thought can't control
To draw me back with your love enduring.
 The pages that speak of our own consignment
 Can never depress us in their confinement.

Sonnet No. 93

There is awesome power in the mind of Man,
Which can be potent enough to overcome
Our natural drive to be but charlatan;
So angel/devil seeks equilibrium.
Though deception seems our inheritance –
To be coeval with our monkey brains –
To be honest is the true elegance
That human intelligence can obtain.
And so, with you dear one, I'll be honest,
For balance is more than just the telling;
The force of your love for me is greatest
When your good my bad is dispelling.
    Let your angel whisper to my devil;
    Shut him up by the strength of your goodwill.

Sonnet No. 94

Nature is the supreme lord example,
And so in every zoo around the world,
Orphaned young are given to the love ample
Only same-sex couples offer unfurled.
A film about the truth of animals
Makes the wide suppression of footage clear;
That all signs of their bond-affectionals
Are censored as one-off shots of the queer.
But, like the egg fostered by the penguin pair,
The truth can be carried to it full term,
And they will teach the others what is fair
Through offspring only Love can reaffirm.
    So do not believe their willful conceit
    To cheat God's plan through human deceit.

Sonnet No. 95

We are only made of matter that dies,
Of bones and marrow; of skull and of brains;
And every thought we had will end in sighs,
As those who bury us mourn our remains.
A Roman mosaic of a skeleton
Shows him toasting fate with pitchers of wine –
His *memento mori* is a ghastly grin
To remind we toil under a heavy fine.
But, finite as the threat hangs on our head,
Our necks are blessed with freedom, and with choice,
For those who have loved can never be dead,
And their thoughts will ever find living voice.
    Horace said *monumentum aere perennius*,
    And meant Love is the bronze tough enough to preserve us.

Sonnet No. 96

The fever may break, but my body's weak –
Racked with fatigue; parched in mouth and spirit;
Thinking in all things I have passed my peak,
If my stubborn will can let me hear it.
Donnie Darko came from Netflix, and now
I have two choices; to watch, or send back.
If that film's darkness I will allow,
Like-cures-like, my sadness it might attack.
No one knows what the day will bring along,
What thoughts or portents we may encounter,
But for this heart, it still carries one song –
And your love inspires its accounter.
    Yet fevered of mind, and weak of body,
    Your smile predicts my sole recovery.

Sonnet No. 97

The way you could not hold my gaze confirms
That there is something wrong, but how to guess
Your reticence is the proof that affirms
Your caring for me is under duress.
The sadness that I can see, and the fear;
The way your eyes dart, and your hand takes mine;
Cannot prepare me for what I'll hear,
When you timidly ask, if I am fine.
My fever caused you more stress than I thought,
And in the hollow of your eyes I see
Halfway between hope and fear you are caught,
For without me, you don't know how you'd be.
    Hand in hand; hold my eye and I'll tell you:
    Leave you is the one thing I'll never do.

Sonnet No. 98

You paused during the Halloween party,
And with the white face paint not able to hide
Your darkness from the swirl of activity,
You leaned on a doorframe, and wished me by your side.
But for me you should not have spoiled your fun,
Though I know it was for but a moment –
Your sparkling thought bears no comparison
When you can gift me with such a bestowment.
And so you rose and rejoined your group again,
A little bit wiser; a bit relieved,
For the refreshment you crave will be there when
The bare idea of my love is conceived.
    Lean on me when you feel the most alone,
    And my strength will be there for you to intone.

Sonnet No. 99

You wonder where I have been your whole life;
Why it was we could not have met more soon,
For it's true I could have eased much of your strife,
And to do so would have been a boon.
Instead of slowing down, now they say
The universe accelerates its rate
As it rips itself apart and won't delay
Inevitable fracture in every state.
But, faith demands that we make decision:
To envision that what happens matters;
Though beyond our understanding's vision,
Acceleration itself falsehood shatters.
    That we met at all is a loving mercy
    From the apparently heartless void we see.

Sonnet n° 100

De marcher rue Cler, à toi ma douce,
Est un doux rêve de Paris, et un jour
Nous verrons ses récoltes dans le bonheur
Avec nos coeurs étincelants en astuce.

Plus tard, ma main sera votre capuce,
Prenant le café dans une arrière-cour –
Celle qui donne cachette sur notre atour,
Ainsi pas à pas nous allons jouir de cette pouce.

Sous les draps blanc comme neige des feuilles,
Tout va faire fondre notre isolement
Comme je m'agenouille pour embrasser la tranquille
Vos lèvres douces magistralement,
Et mutuellement nous allons verrouilles
Sur la musique de ce martèlement.

Sonnet No. 101

Sometimes the draw of this paper is all
I have to pull me out of bed, and think
My lonely snow-white sheets will take the scrawl
Of my restless hope spilling out into ink.
I imagine Zhivago, and the ice
He had to chop through to get to his desk,
But – the unfrozen chamber must entice –
For at its center, lays love picturesque.
Alone with my sheets, I draw you out too;
I write your name at the top of my heart,
And allow icy blood the ink to bestrew,
For every word is drawn before I start.
    Alone within my center chamber room,
    Love predestines with Its fiery plume.

Sonnet No. 102

Two young men locked in a tender embrace
Were buried together in ancient times –
One supports on his chest his beloved's face,
And archeologists lauded their finds.
'Romantic!' the scientists said freely:
An example of marital devotion
That even death could not cheat completely,
And which can yet stir human emotion.
But, this tale has not a happy ending,
For they thought man and woman were so interred,
And to the love of men they went denying –
The truth before their eyes with fresh dirt inured.
    To deny the basic truth of Love cheats,
    And all of human intellect defeats.

Sonnet No. 103

Too often we might forget, communion
Is in the heart of communication –
And in its way, so too is discipline
Lost in the force of deliberation.
But content can be abstractly charted,
Like dolphin song on an X-Y layout,
Though we won't speak it, knowledge is imparted,
For the forty-five-degree cant leaves no doubt.
So too, expressions of love are genuine
When they don't fall to generalization –
And they can plot all the meaning herein
That points to substance without hesitation.
    What language may yet try to discover,
    Love's intuition can always uncover.

Sonnet No. 104

The other night, when you teased me and went to bed,
Did you really think I'd prefer my TV show,
And not trail you to where your silent footsteps led? –
Oh no, from the bedroom doorway I watched you go,
And settle yourself like a leaf upon the sheets;
One moment, eyes to the light, the next gliding down,
For every inch your body a graceful arc meets
When your head finally makes my pillow your crown.
But, it was the smile that you turned on me right then,
With its blend of love and observation,
That told me our best lovemaking would soon begin,
So I stepped to you in calm exhilaration.
    I too felt like I was a falling leaf,
    Settling on your body in disbelief.

Sonnet No. 105

Bundled in grayness, clouds become your coat –
You step out into the autumn's day and
Cast eyes skyward; tug a scarf 'round your throat –
For here conserved warmth takes the season's stand.
I love to see you prepped, just like a child,
Going out for a day of harvest work,
With clothes rigid, but with expression mild,
For apple-picking time we must not shirk.
And later, with our fruit and our labor,
Sweet cinnamon will lace our pies and sauce
So that our smiles and flatware may savor
Feeding the other by scooping his gloss.
    So the day begins, and already ends;
    Smiles and bright moods sheer happiness portends.

Sonnet No. 106

Safe in the folds of fiery autumn's glitter,
A painter nestled his private studio,
Where over and over he had one sitter
Gaze the landscape, while he built her folio.
'Helga,' for whom this shack was built, gazes out,
With the serenity only Love sees,
And will always live in His vision devout,
Though the world burn up, or totally freeze.
So too I cast about with words my paint
To reflect upon you, with reflected grace,
The hope the future won't think these are faint,
But through Love will be able to see your face.
    Hills may yet roll, in the ever-shifting fire,
    But return perennial, to new inspire.

Sonnet No. 107

When I'm sick or lonely, I have a need
As basic as bedrock shelter and food,
Though the last thing I'd want to plead
Is pity for a baleful attitude.
Pride should not be boastful, for if it is,
The allotment of your gift for me trumps
All the sureties of answers and quiz,
For without it, they put me in the dumps.
I know you love me, that's not in question,
Yet I'm sometimes ill and isolated
Within the confines of my own body's skin,
So just say it, if you feel I'm agitated.
    Like music to soothe the savage breast's wounding,
    Your words of love cure me by their attuning.

Sonnet No. 108

How can I approach 116 and not
Have trepidation by analogy?
Though time changes Love not one single blot,
Incomplete art deserves apology.
Beloved as I may be, my remover
Compasses Love in His most perfect form,
To convert doubter to true believer –
To behold His bright star through every storm.
And so, you and I are married in mind,
Although your height outpaces mine by inches,
I've taken it, and by it others will find
The concrete measure that their own clinches.
    Just know, it is no error we were meant to love,
    God with divider proportions all from above.

Sonnet No. 109

If I pluck from the air a question old,
I'm sure that many will know what I mean,
For universally in this state bold,
One's love in another's is easily seen.
So shall I write how beautiful you are? –
How your eyes sparkle with wit and pleasure;
How your face is that of an angel's boudoir
Where my happy thoughts constantly seek leisure.
Shall I say what it is like to take your hand? –
To feel the firmness, and reciprocation,
As you hold me back from your firebrand,
But pull mine closer, for some compensation.
    Back and forth, there may be some gentle tussle,
    But it's always good to stretch Love's muscle.

Sonnet No. 110 [4]

To walk Rue Cler, with you my bright sweetheart,
Is a sweet dream of Paris, and one day
We'll view its produce gathered in outlay
With hearts effervescent and sparkling smart.

And later my hand will play your cap's part,
Having coffee in a court hidden away –
Over-watched by the bedchamber where we stay,
And to it, step by step, every inch we'll chart.

Under linens as white as sheets of snow,
All our sense of isolation will melt,
As I kneel there to kiss the tranquil glow
Off your soft lips so masterfully felt,
And mutually we will lock on so
To the music which that hammering dealt.

Sonnet No. 111

What intimidates more than a blank page? –
'Different' is far from complimentary,
But at least a comment's something to gauge
Better than apathy sedentary.
Yet, why let them bother me? – I'll push aside
The fact they shut down a wish to engage,
And instead pull to me my object of pride;
The fact of your love is strong tutelage.
Let your heart their lackluster lives upstage,
As your conjured image warms my passion,
But mellows my temper through gentle swage,
While teaching them to love after our fashion.
    In emptiness is also potential;
    And the will to fight every obstacle.

Sonnet No. 112

In the space I laid out for me to write,
A terrier paw bid me make him room –
So I shoved aside my art for you tonight,
And in place of sonnets, his comforts assume.
Nestling my chin on his fur, I extol
Your lovely Gina – pure white Angora –
Whose tender azure gaze touches your soul,
To let you see my blue eyes incognita.
But now, a happy kiss brushes my nose,
For the love that's in hand is always bliss,
The truth of which every Airedale knows,
When contact is joy beyond analysis.
    In Gina see my calm when you look at her,
    And in my dog, I'll feel your devotion stir.

Sonnet No. 113 [5]

Mendelssohn wrote his lovely *Songs without Words*,
Where harmony alone carries content –
And this vibe from a cold sleep came by thirds
To wake with its pulse by ardent intent.
Sometimes feeling alone is the message,
And word following word just lets it flow;
Like a fugue, both on fire and on edge,
One must let it work, so that it may go.
If melody in this is allowed to sing,
Lyrics or not, there's one theme keeps the time,
And maybe to some, it alone is the thing
That justifies art, and this paltry rhyme.
    For love of you, I trade sleep for impression
    And the beat of heart seeking expression.

Sonnet No. 114

I would like some feedback on this effort –
Not from you, dear boy, for you I know I please,
But from others I find I crave report
That my fire in their chill heart can play and tease.
For warmth between humans is connection,
And without it, the divine spark we have
Glints cold and distant with no relation
To ache in pain without that healing salve.
So I would seek, dear boy, to know if they care,
And have a sentiment as real as this –
For if not, they do not hunt it anywhere,
If not in how I feel about you, Tony.
    This burns so that human hearts may kindle
    A passion like ours not meant to dwindle.

Sonnet No. 115

Attuned to Nature, and to worlds of loss,
One young man's sorrow was consigned to record
Tears from birds – from beast and plants, and even moss –
For Orpheus struck his lyre most lyrichord.
Then, another young man tossed furniture
Out his bedroom window, so that the poor
Might feel Saint Francis a fellow voyager
In a world whose inequities need uproar.
Thus, Orpheus struck a chord and waited,
And Saint Francis offered a stigmata –
While to both, Nature came safe and sated
To attend their human serenata.
　　With afflicted palm opened then towards the sky,
　　I offer song and prayer, and you're the reason why.

Sonnet No. 116

Often it seems sorrow are the lyrics,
Coursing beneath my metres' beating strain –
Slipping; sliding – not able to affix
Scope or compass to my doleful refrain.
But, it's not as if I'm sad, exactly,
No, if anything, it's a deep desire
To feed this sense of joy most compactly
In form to make me its justifier.
These words may now exist because of me,
But the soul that surges through them is you –
Take one away and there's nothing to see,
'Cept the music diffuse making them true.
　　Not set in time, but measuring out,
　　My love drums, and about you wants to flout!

Sonnet No. 117

Oh my darling, come lay your touch on me –
Let it drift and linger, and your smile say
That this is the way it will always be,
In spite of change, or place, or time of day.
The kitchen table's bare without you there –
No elbows on the wood, and no laughter,
For on cold mornings like this, it's not fair
That I face a day this much emptier.
But, on the table is laid out this thought –
To gather me your pausing touch and feel,
Your pressure with timbre of voice is brought,
To hold and remind that your love's real.
    Near or far, our separations are brief;
    Although apart, never is our belief.

Sonnet No. 118

In beauty's eye, every generation
Comes to bear with just the same potential –
Which explains with youth our fascination,
And its blessings and curse exponential.
But then, what means any of that, I ask,
When looking in a crib upon the smile
Of a little one in whose love to bask,
And who will shoulder our hopes for awhile.
Although we are creatures of flesh and bone,
We are also ones of hope and spirit;
With desires not to be alone
When soul this body must decide to quit.
    So please join with me that we might also
    All the joys and pain of fatherhood know.

Sonnet No. 119

So often I see the handsome young men,
Whose fair features put me in mind of you,
And I might long to whisper to them then
Their beauty reminds me of *your* divine cue.
But if you see my glance, don't be jealous;
If you see me waver under their view,
Know their loveliness is just a trellis
Where I can plant the sweetest thoughts of you.
Once known, the marriage of beauty and soul
Will not stand the weight of one, it's true,
But together, one the other must extol,
So I borrow beauty in tribute of you.
    Though passing features may cause a tremble,
    Only your face, my heart, can resemble.

Sonnet No. 120

Before the Supreme Court stood – Edie Windsor –
On her breast, her wife's proud diamond 'ring' still blazed,
Forty-six years after Edie was first dazed
That the woman she loved was proposing to her.
A private woman, the press she would endure
To end bigotry, and all were amazed,
Telling a great love story, she was not fazed,
For it was time for justice to transfer.
Love endures, thus diamonds are the symbol –
Tough too, like Edie and her spouse, you'll mind
Through the nagging dinge of Time, are able
To hold partners tight; not to choke, nor bind,
    But in the way I love you, they stable
    The hand on heart that can forever find.

Sonnet No. 121

Who among us will stop to consider
The pull of the crush; the ordinary;
And the pulsing shot of the calendar
Witnessed through slots of the momentary.
In a joy not many can understand,
I like to shop the day before Thanksgiving –
The Wednesday evening supermarket, and,
Those hurried and harried pull my heartstring.
For these are of the moments no one writes,
What slips common purpose of sympathy
Farther away from the will that recites
The dull, dead fade slipping to apathy.
    But – Wednesday night, let's stand with laced fingers,
    And feel bound through love to all those strangers.

Sonnet No. 122

Love is a buoy that floats, that can lift
Deepest thoughts from the bottom of despair –
Love is the anchor stopping boats adrift
From letting their keels wander unaware.
So drowsy, my eyes want to close, but don't,
For in their searing state through the darkness,
Starlight sought is the one thing that I won't
Have any chance to meet with like success.
With line cast on your marker, on your bell,
My bow points to safety and to harbor,
Where in port, perhaps I can rest a spell,
Once sky/water; hope/destiny might blur.
    Dreams fix me and make me a permanent mark –
    O Love, raise a great star from my feeble spark.

Sonetto N. 123

Mi manchi come le tegole manca la pioggia,
e che la sete può essere
vissuto come pene delle ere
scendendo a bagnare l'alloggia.

Qui di seguito ho disalloggia,
voci sommesse dicono: 'amittere,'
ma non voglio evitare del bufere,
per il paesaggio non ha foggia.

  Invece io e te coccole
  dal fuoco, sotto una coperta
  così il nostro vino abbondevole
  ci sentiamo alcuna malcerta
  durante il nostro accarezzandole
  come nell'amore ci sono erta.

Sonnet No. 124

You ask my love to be ever more perfect,
But I know of you I cannot ask the same –
For I feel what tumult that would affect,
And in your ire, you'd say I was to blame.
Do you know what most this paper is like? –
A pressing of chopped little bits construed,
Ground down and soaked till it has no more bite,
Because in blank form, no one thinks it's rude.
So, my love can take the ink of you, boy,
Lay down upon my back your demands, and see,
I show the best way for you to deploy
A flawless love that with yours can agree.
If I make but one claim upon you, know –
It is that your love continue to grow.

Sonnet No. 125

I will lay me down one sheet at a time,
For you are master-poet of my heart,
When the humble form of me as your rhyme
Twains a start with an end that will not part.
Only your true words of love are music
To a soul in fear that such things can fade,
For like a beast, I crave the most basic
Strains of but the sweetest joy to be played.
But, alas – now I know I ask too much;
Set me up for a fall I will regret;
Yet hope, damn him, will always seek a touch
To beat back annihilation's hungry threat.
   So I circle back to nowhere again –
   And perhaps did nothing but drain my pen.

Sonnet No. 126

I want to overrun your defenses,
Rush at your walls till they come tumbling down,
Till my trumpet blast, soft as a murmur says,
You can't resist the greatness of my renown.
In many ways, my boy is now a man,
For pride rises to consider your strength
Like a fatherly boast that it was my plan
To bring you thus far, so you'd go the whole length.
As I storm and win your love and self-control,
You cede to me everything that matters –
Your mind, your heart, and your body and soul,
And there I leave your false fronts in tatters,
   Not a victory for me alone,
   But for you, it proves how you have grown.

Sonnet No. 127

Poetry kindles itself on two fires –
Blows two breaths upon cinders divided,
For either hope or despair it inspires
To flame and make the lonely feel invited.
In your spirit's glow, I know you're ready,
For December buzzes within your heart,
Making the stress of the passing year petty
Compared to knowing we won't be apart.
So with *glögg* and pulled-up throw, let's snuggle –
Before the crackling fire, we will know,
One part must be warm for the cold to struggle,
And on your entire love, heat bestow.
    With our kissing breath, we fuel just one flame;
    Eternity will feel it just the same.

Sonnet No. 128

Slip your waiting little hand in mine, for –
Though chilled by bleak winter's taunt – I know how
A warming touch thrills when it's full of ardor;
If my fingers, your glove, you will allow.
So we go walking thorough the bright chill air,
Swinging interlocked hands down the sidewalk,
While your knit cap rakishly shows some hair,
Pulling you close for an intimate talk.
Your smile dies to see me fall on one knee:
"Baby, I love you; what time is there to waste? –
Marry me to bind two hearts, and set them free."
Yet – your blinking says I've acted in haste.
    My cheeks in your hands, you force me to rise,
    Where your nod and tears says 'yes' from your eyes.

Sonnet No. 129

Love is a flow that many try to staunch;
Think in that triage they do themselves good –
In granting childish fears total *carte blanche* –
So good intentions are misunderstood.
I awoke to find your head upon my chest,
And in the morning light, you slept lullaby
To the sound you say soothes you now the best,
So I stroked your brow while you heard my heart sigh.
We are beyond the fear others prop up
And use to keep themselves isolated,
For in us there is a seamless link-up,
Knowing Love's never late or belated.
    I let your peaceful dream play out today,
    For tomorrow's tomorrow is on its way.

Sonnet No. 130

Melodies are these: ones with three refrains –
    In whose structure I find total freedom,
    Where my small mind can be adventuresome,
Stacking high a couplet with three quatrains.
Yet, my praise of one, its partner attains –
    Like lovers whose equalities become
    His husband's settled equilibrium,
And in that mutual support, Love sustains.
        So with liberty to go where I please,
        My destination always finds one spot
        Upon your person to tickle and tease,
        For in your pleasure I find that I'm not
        A man who with his freedom is at ease,
        Unless with your image and love besot.

Sonnet No. 131

As a man engaged, I may see the world
Where differences are insignificant,
And every slander that was ever hurled
Is rendered mute by Love, and irrelevant.
In you can I offer me salvation,
For every act of self-love is forgiving –
Like handfuls of dirt without hesitation
To inter dead flesh by the living.
In you, there's chance to rise incorruptible
Though my body to that sleep must take its turn,
These words, tenacious and incorrigible,
Will live in Love and continue to learn.
    Heart-by-heart, their deliverance will teach me,
    By loving you, infinity I'll see.

Sonnet No. 132

To draw a piece of paper and then write
Poetry of form set, but intent soft,
Makes goal to your intellect and heart delight,
And all the cares you carry to be sloughed.
I make no more demands on your love, but –
From now on it will be fault-free; innocent,
Like your purity of breath, it's clear-cut
To reward me with boundless nourishment.
Let me take the burdens from your shoulders;
Let me massage them, and let my lips stray,
For verse is limited as enfolders
Of your arms and chest, and what I must say.
    "I love you" is whispered into your flesh,
    Where your sigh redeems poetry afresh.

Sonnet No. 133

When you are tired and your muscles ache;
When the day's stress rides hard on neck and blades,
Lay yourself down, and your burdens forsake,
While I light candles that your bad mood dissuades.
Over your tense form my fingers make a stake
To claim the right to mine with no withholder;
To drain from your worries by daybreak,
So you will dazzle every beholder.
But the night has just begun to awake,
And the candles' scent in our brain smolders –
Raise your arms, and let my hands undertake
To massage you, and melt our composure.
    And if a stray kiss lands perchance here and there,
    You'll find my bargain's payment is more than fair.

Sonnet No. 134

Time is short, and it grows ever fleeting
With a million voices speaking at once
For attention; for hate; for love; seeking
To stop destiny's crush that Man confronts.
Sometimes I see me picking up a book,
Where end-papers have 'born and dead' brackets,
Squeezing the author to the course his life took,
Negating all that he was and transmits.
So, how not to bend to soul-crushing fate? –
For if I saw my own lived/died timeline,
How could it then any more motivate
My impassioned drive to fortune outshine?
    Yet, our voice won't perish, because the truth,
    And Love, speaks clearly to the heart of youth.

Sonnet No. 135

In our genes is what makes us who we are;
The initials decoded as roadmap
Marks our journey's path as an avatar,
But in the info's void, souls overlap.
The Master Geneticist planned it so,
And no Frankenstein tinkering should be
Man's hubris and bigoted Jim Crow
'Gainst our Maker's plan, that they plainly see.
But, you and I can smile in our "D 'n' A,"
For you plus me equals God's distinction,
And His granting of Love upon the day
We wed will be His chart's true completion.
    To the letters that make up you and I,
    We have His initials blessing our tie.

Sonnet No. 136

As we trim the tree, let's take a moment
To act like the kids we feel deep inside,
For sparkle lies between each ornament,
And hand-in-hand, we'll see its underside.
When a boy, I would lie beneath the tree
So my eyes could drift up the greenwood trunk;
Where blinking lights lit the holiday esprit;
While my cares and woes to the background shrunk.
Lying here now with you, our biceps set
One against the other, your lips whisper:
"I used to do this too, but I won't forget
This moment and exactly where we were."
    My eyes slowly close on the beauty above,
    To treasure your shining kiss of purest love.

Sonnet No. 137

The small tree upstairs, we can see from our bed –
Saffron, vermilion, amber and blue lights
Play about your smile; my hand on your head,
As your gaze to me relays their delights.
So, sorrow is out of place, and yet there,
For the number of Christmases we'll know
Is already set and logged-in somewhere,
And adds a somber cast to the scene's glow.
You sense what I feel, as you always do;
Caressing my cheek, you say: "It's all right,"
And there with your love, I know what is true –
The glint of infinity is in sight.
    Those colored lights also strobe with our hearts,
    And in your eyes, every sadness departs.

Sonnet No. 138

My troubles pile up like bills in a stack.
I take the top one and give it release –
Yet it gives no comfort as I fall back
To the mound that only seems to increase.
I may be far from the man that you think,
But my faults you see; my faults you forgive,
And though they sometimes drive you to the brink,
You comfort me with love intuitive.
My limitations you just take in stride,
And remind me of finer qualities –
You gently hint that I'd better not hide
My boundless love 'neath such frivolities.
    Like bills, troubles come and go like the leaves,
    But your love pays every debt and reprieves.

Sonnet No. 139

I joke as I tousle your hair in bed
That I had better pin you to the top
Of our Christmas tree as angel instead
Of the star that but plays the tired prop.
Buying that tree together, you and I,
The man at the lot approached us on par,
Calling us "Folks," to in that testify
He saw two men in love – just as we are!
From bed we watch the tree, as we do now,
While the lights burn softly in reflection,
Your angelic goodness outshines somehow
That tinsel gold and painted perfection.
    You are my sign/symbol of the season,
    For in your love, beauty finds its reason.

Sonnet No. 140 [6]

I miss you like the tiles miss the rain,
in whose very thirst is allowed admit
of longing like that of the ages fit
to free-fall and wet down the house like pain.

Below I am a person thrown out like Cain,
urged by soft voices saying: 'accept it,'
but, I won't be driven by storms to quit,
for the landscape has no shape on its plane.

    Instead, together we'll draw, and cuddle
    near to the fire, under our blanket,
    with our red wine flowing most abounding;
    where all uncertainty we'll befuddle
    caressing such under the coverlet,
    and find in love all that is ascending.

Sonnet No. 141

Like a curtain of scintillating sheath,
The ones and zeros of reality
Matrix themselves flatly in our belief,
Then settle in forms of finality.
Hindus conceive of all experience
As being set down upon the pages
Of Akashic knowledge that we may reference,
If our hearts are pure enough for the ages.
And so in living code I have writ you
Large in the great book with its sacred seal,
Whose transparent veil can only be seen through
With the holy eyes of Love that know what's real.
    For all times our love will be recorded –
    Kept safe, treasured, and by like-minds, hoarded.

Sonnet No. 142

As it ticks its arbitrary passage,
The new year's countdown makes me think of them –
All those young men, and the time they bridge –
For their beauty stays, though the years condemn.
And you and I? – How will we remember
The fullness of this vanishing moment,
From the vantage of many years' number,
Together for the lifetime that we've spent?
Youth may fade, but perennial as New Years,
The fresh-faced count replenishes like grass –
The trick is finding one without tears
To accept and allow the years to pass.
    Two dozen days like this have we in store,
    So, let's toast the old with new evermore.

Sonnet No. 143

On that day, I'll see you standing in white –
Your tux a badge of the office we seek –
With four hands linked, we'll take the nuptial rite
To cross Love's threshold, with its bright mystique.
But I blink – and the day's already here –
Your fingers grip mine; the officiator
Asks you the simple question loud and clear:
Do you take me? Forever, in *amour?*
"I do." you say, and your heart is sincere.
My turn comes, and my black tux speaks symbol
Of our gravity, and of permanence;
Of our life together, and of love nimble
That will guide us to our death from here hence.
    "I do," I say to you with a firm glance,
    And take the pride of a married man's stance.

Sonnet No. 144

I am but one man against the flow of Time,
And after I am dead, others will label
What they see in me with words that are not mine;
Thus, homophobes will give full rein to their libel.
Even now, the 'H' word is jammed down our throats,
As Wikipedia gives haters free roam –
To define us with a word that gets our goats –
As if Blacks were called 'negroes' in that tome!
What I call myself is the all-important,
Because I do it with love, and therefore,
How sad that I'll be in their hands ignorant,
When I cannot defend myself anymore.
    So to future bigots of the world, I say:
    Hate yourself with the 'H-word,' for I am Gay.

Sonnet No. 145

Sometimes the will alone is like flying –
A feathered thing, that soars above our cares –
And the Truth never feels like denying
The one-by-one steps that up-climb Love's stairs.
On the plane you sleep, with head on my arm,
While out the window, we're above the clouds,
For in your slumber passes by all harm,
Like a dream ship with cotton candy shrouds.
When you wake, we'll be on our honeymoon –
Though the destination I've kept secret –
Our vows we will re-commit very soon
Where modern lovers, ancient loves beget.
    So fly your dreams without care as I keep
    Vigil sound to protect you as you sleep.

Sonnet No. 146

What's inspiration, if not restlessness? –
A mental itch always seeking a scratch
And a way to deal with thoughts in excess
Of feelings binding them in sharp crosshatch.
So here in the early morning quiet,
With my pen bespeaking my impatience,
The fact that I can't sleep, I try to forget,
With the joy that we are now relations.
For motion's the better part of movement,
And the patterns I lay down have momentum –
For the present with the future has blent,
And my actions speak, though my tongue is dumb.
    You and I have overlaid heart and soul,
    And that design I've no wish to control.

Sonnet No. 147

Weeds grow between the stones; the sun burns hot;
So watch your footing as we scale the mount,
For up here, the sea is in earshot,
And the glories of Greece under us we'll count.
To the tomb of Iolaus, outside Thebes,
I have taken you like ancient men did,
To marry in the name of Hercules,
On his husband's grave, there-joined by Cupid.
For that lad to his man was charioteer,
And three hundred Sacred Band partners too –
Each a warrior couple – married here,
Pledging to die, and live, as one man through.
    So on the grassy stones, let's links our hands –
    And fulfill our vow as ancient rite demands.

Sonnet No. 148

Emotions jostle the road like judgments,
To form a pack of wheeled carts there pushing
Ruts ever deeper in worn resentments;
Where none but accusations go whooshing.
Yet, calmly within the tumult's jarring,
The source of my best inspiration comes,
With gentle grasp, and on his finger, a ring –
And in whose touch, my mute questions, he numbs.
Knowing we are but one man can settle
The disquiet of my rough intellect,
For absolving through Love has greater mettle
Than my self-damning torment can subject.
    Reach to me this morning, and caress my cheek;
    Your love has all the comfort I'll ever seek.

Sonnet No. 149

Is there anything as warm as a human smile? –
A thing more endeared to greater felicity;
That can turn on one with the warmth of the sun's style;
Or a safer place to build domesticity?
Awake the day, my husband, with your kind beaming –
Show the sun just what paradise is like,
And melt my cares like some vapors scheming
To creep over the sill of my heart and strike.
For this morning, the sun is rising in my arms –
And I can see my soul is made but nothing of
The reflected gold bright enough to erase harms,
And also mirror back to me a face in love.
Let us build a home for one another in there,
And be settled down, no matter how, when, or where.

Sonnet No. 150

The day awaits, so let's embrace it, dear –
　　Let our bed sheet fly to every corner,
　　So to the night past, we're not a mourner,
But with sails set, to our delights we'll steer.

To you, warrior, I'm charioteer –
　　An Apollo to your bright blazoner,
　　And to your worship, a practitioner,
For my knight, you are my brave cavalier!

　　　So up with you already, dearest boy,
　　　The hours of our roving await us,
　　　And with Fate itself, we'll find we can toy,
　　　As our kisses greet sky in perfect buss,
　　　Then pause a moment, stilled by quiet joy,
　　　To make the clouds and flowers envious.

Sonnet No. 151

The dogs sport at our feet with playful jaws,
While your Gina eyes them from cool detachment.
Grooming her Angora fur with licked claws,
You are proud that she is independent.
On the windowsill quickly sprouts your gift,
The paperwhite bulbs to brighten winter,
And prove with sweet fragrance our minds can lift
Like daffodils to be gray weather's tinter.
Side-by-side on the sofa, we survey
The kingdom of our love's prosperity,
While in my silent heart, I humbly pray
The home we build will be of equity.
    Let my hand plant into yours, and then know,
    We're soil enough for the other to grow.

Sonnet No. 152

After a trying day, Love's a warm bath,
Whose firm support presses, but does not crush
The child in me He knows is an empath,
And able to feel his purest uprush.
The water of Love is like liquid jewels,
Ground and pulverized by work-a-day strain,
But in that diamond-crush are shattered the rules
That sorrow is an emotion to refrain.
So, with you, I slip beneath the waters,
Knowing my soaked head will rise to behold
Your head be-doused with sparkling gem starters
At the other end of the tub so bold.
    To that matrix let me add a single tear,
    The one I can brush from your cheek without fear.

Sonnet No. 153

The tarpaulin is spread upon the floor,
And our meager dinner comes from a box –
Yet stillness rules from roof to corridor,
While we share our bagels, cream cheese and lox.
You chew, and I recall our trudging home
With paint cans, and a new color we approve,
To make this old place not mine, but our own,
And this moment's beauty we can't improve.
For sometimes the greatest intensity
Comes not from the strongest of exertion,
But from the ordinary banality
Of a quiet moment in full immersion.
    Love in climax is no different than now,
    Where in candlelight your features endow.

Sonnet No. 154 (7)

Content like the partners where they reside
Within Steven Walker's loving paintings,
You and I find the peace where we confide
The dignity of low-toned acquaintings.
His men are settled within their own space,
Where the everyday world stops its pressure;
Where spouses create their own state of grace,
And the love they live spreads out fresh and sure.
So different from David Hockney's landscape,
Where men in pairs seen never more alone,
And more desiring of an escape,
Because to self-hate, I guess, they are prone.
    The world we make is one of solemn promise,
    Soft-eyed to imbue us, and the world, with bliss.

Sonnet No. 155

Now we have what we need, but I desire
The final and greatest gift you can give –
That our joined name can live on and inspire
The love we have formed, and our lives outlive.
Carried forth in the world, we'll be proud fathers,
Knowing each generation will make it
Easier for our kind, for as grandfathers,
They'll teach Love, not hate, and with us will prove it.
The lessons our kids will know in their hearts
Will be passed in our name and memory,
And shall outshine the luster of my arts
To place our love in the heart of history.
    So I ask you humbly to give us a son,
    And in your offspring, all my work is done.

Text Notes

(1) Sonnet No. 19: For Rick and Ren's great love story, see my essay on the topic here:

https://gayauthors.org/blogs/entry/13701-in-the-flesh-homophobia-and-the-zombie-menace/

(2) Sonnet No. 40: Translation of *Sono e pensoso*, Sonetto 35 dal *Rerum vulgarium fragmenta* di Francesco Petrarca. Published in November of 1337.

Solo e pensoso, i più deserti campi,
Vo mesurando a passi tardi e lenti;
E gli occhi porto per fuggire intenti
Ove vestigio uman l'arena stampi.
Altro schermo non trovo che mi scampi
Dal manifesto accorger de le genti;
Perchè negli atti d'allegrezza spenti
Di fuor si legge com'io dentro avampi.
  Sì ch'io mi credo omai che monti et piagge
  E fiumi e selve sappian di che tempre
  Sia la mia vita, ch'è celata altrui.
  Ma pur sì aspre vie nè sì selvagge
  Cercar non so, ch'Amor non venga sempre
  Ragionando con meco, et io co llui.

(3) Sonnet No. 90: Translation of *Il mio abbraccio ti aspetta*, Sonetto N. 80 above.

(4) Sonnet No. 110: Translation of *De marcher rue Cler, à toi ma douce*, Sonnet n° 100 above.

(5) Sonnet No. 113: Written as lyrics for Mendelssohn's *Songs without Words*, Op.30, No. 3 in E Major. A partial recapitulation of the second subject is necessary to accommodate the couplet.

https://www.youtube.com/watch?v=5RJ9vHBZIFs

(6) Sonnet No. 140: Translation of *Mi manchi come la tegole*, Sonetto N. 123 above.

(7) Sonnet 154: See Steve Walker's paintings here:

https://www.facebook.com/Steve-Walker-Fine-Art-349510928797011/

www.ingramcontent.com/pod-product-compliance
Lightning Source LLC
LaVergne TN
LVHW051015080826
845145LV00009B/2644

* 9 7 8 1 9 5 3 3 8 9 1 0 7 *